# EXPLORING EARTH'S BIOMES

Claire O'Neal

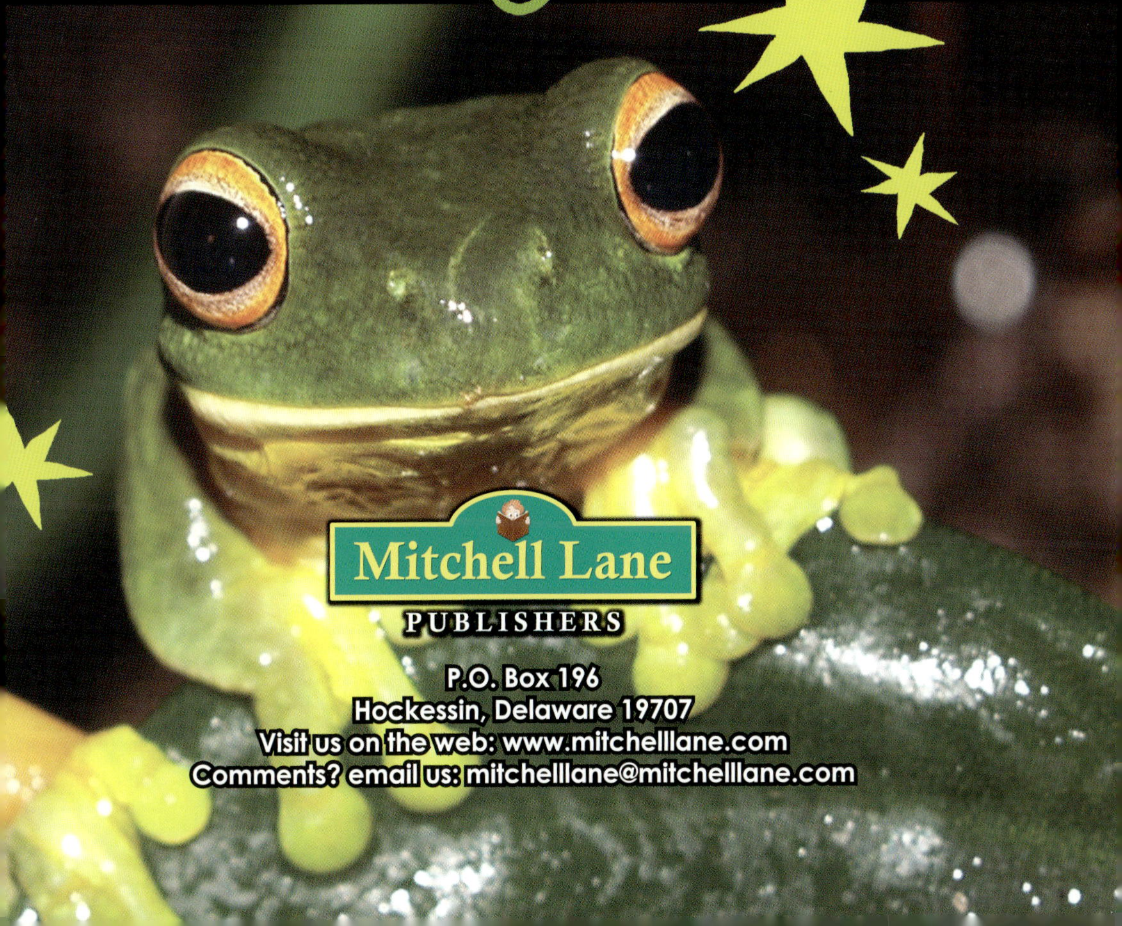

Mitchell Lane
PUBLISHERS

P.O. Box 196
Hockessin, Delaware 19707
Visit us on the web: www.mitchelllane.com
Comments? email us: mitchelllane@mitchelllane.com

**A Project Guide to:**
**Exploring Earth's Biomes** • Fish and Amphibians
Mammals • Projects in Genetics • Reptiles and Birds
Sponges, Worms, and Mollusks

Copyright © 2011 by Mitchell Lane Publishers

All rights reserved. No part of this book may be reproduced without written permission from the publisher. Printed and bound in the United States of America.

PUBLISHER'S NOTE: The facts on which the story in this book is based have been thoroughly researched. Documentation of such research can be found on page 45. While every possible effort has been made to ensure accuracy, the publisher will not assume liability for damages caused by inaccuracies in the data, and makes no warranty on the accuracy of the information contained herein.

Library of Congress Cataloging-in-Publication Data

O'Neal, Claire.
  Exploring earth's biomes / Claire O'Neal.
    p. cm. — (Life science projects for kids)
  Includes bibliographical references and index.
  ISBN 978-1-58415-878-3 (library bound)
  1. Biotic communities. I. Title.
  QH541.14.O52 2011
  577—dc22
                                    2010034850

Printing  1  2  3  4  5  6  7  8  9
                                    PLB

# CONTENTS

Introduction ..................................................... 4

Tundra: Survival of the Insulated ........................ 8

Taiga: Land of the Conifer ................................ 10

Rain Forest: Competition .................................. 14

Temperate Deciduous Forest: Hibernation ........ 18

Grassland: Fighting Erosion .............................. 22

Desert: Thirsty Plants ....................................... 26

Biomes in a Bag ............................................... 30

Hula Hoop Biomes ........................................... 32

Food Web: Where Does Your Dinner
  Come From? .................................................. 36

Microbe Food Web: Create a
  Winogradsky Column ..................................... 40

Further Reading ............................................... 44

　　Books ......................................................... 44

　　On the Internet ........................................... 44

　　Works Consulted ......................................... 45

Glossary .......................................................... 46

Index ............................................................... 47

# INTRODUCTION

In a quiet mountain range, a bumblebee hovers over purple heather spilling from bare rock. A shaggy mountain goat bleats nearby as it munches the scrubby plants. Chewing lazily, the goat doesn't hear the marmot screeching in warning from inside its gravelly burrow. Feeling a moment's panic too late, the goat collapses as muscular limbs enfold its shaggy body from behind. With a single bite from crushing jaws, the fight is over—the attacking mountain lion has broken the goat's spinal cord. After the goat is ripped to shreds and the lion's belly is full, eagles and vultures spiral downward, scrapping for leftovers. Bacteria living in the sparse soil break down what's left of the goat's carcass. In several months, the scene will once again be a blank canvas of rock and scrub. This is a biome, where every day brings a new struggle to survive.

Biomes are communities of plants and animals that live and die together within a geographic setting. Biomes can be diverse, perhaps supporting many different species of plants and animals in a lush jungle. They can also be sparse, constrained by difficult conditions such as drought or extreme cold. Biologists define six land biomes based on global patterns of temperature and rainfall.

**Tundra** is found in polar regions or in high mountain elevations. These locations are bitter cold year-round, with dry and wet seasons.

*A snowy owl takes flight on the tundra.*

Birds and insects can live there in the summer, but only well-adapted mammals can survive the harsh winter. Vegetation includes short, sparse plants such as shrubs, grasses, lichens, and mosses.

**Taiga** is the largest biome, lying between 50 degrees north latitude and the Arctic Circle. It experiences very cold winters with short days, and pleasant summers with long days. Moisture varies throughout the year. Summer brings insects and birds, but in the winter, only dense conifer forests populated by moose, wolves, and foxes remain.

**Rain forest** biomes can be tropical around the equator, but temperate rain forests are also found at higher latitudes, such as in the Pacific Northwest of the United States or the west coast of New Zealand. Rain forest biomes experience abundant rainfall most of the year, supporting rich plant growth and high species diversity.

**Temperate deciduous forests** are found in the eastern United States, Europe, Russia, China, and Japan. These forests experience four seasons, with cold winters, warm summers, and a low amount of year-round rainfall. The milder winters support plants, mammals, birds, and cold-blooded animals year-round.

**Grasslands,** which occupy 25 percent of the earth's land, are found in the central United States, Argentina, South Africa, and southern

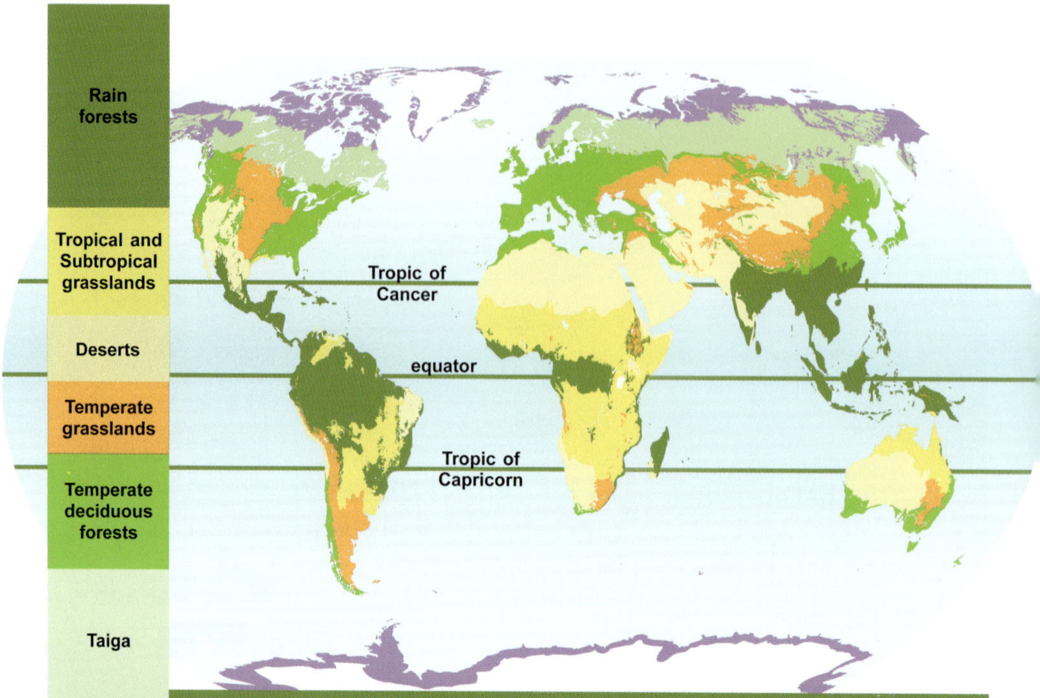

# Exploring Earth's Biomes

Rain forests

Tropical and Subtropical grasslands

Deserts

Temperate grasslands

Temperate deciduous forests

Taiga

Tundra

*There are six major land biomes around the world. Some, such as grasslands, can be tropical or temperate. There are also aquatic biomes, including pond, lake, river, and ocean biomes.*

Russia. This biome experiences cold winters and hot summers, with most rainfall in the spring, helping grasses take root.

**Deserts** are mostly found around the Tropics of Capricorn and Cancer, making up 20 percent of the earth's land. They experience less than 10 inches (25 centimeters) of rainfall throughout the year, with cool winters, hot summers, and an extreme range in daily temperatures. Antarctica is also a major world desert. It remains cold and dry year-round.

The boundaries of the earth's biomes have not always been the same. Over geologic time, the locations of biomes changed as the continents moved or as the climate changed. Plants and animals are completely at the mercy of their changing environment. Living things must either adapt to survive or face extinction.

In this book, you will explore the challenges each biome presents for survival. Conduct fascinating experiments and build working models

# Introduction

to investigate concepts in plant and animal adaptations. Though simple to set up, each experiment encourages you to think like a scientist, asking questions and providing ideas to take your understanding to the next level. Most experiments use materials you probably already have at home. Some experiments ask you to work with **an adult** for safety.

Of all Earth's organisms, humans are one of the most adaptable species. We can live in almost any land-based biome. Because of this, our power to impact the Earth is both awesome and frightening. Many ecologists believe that humans are changing the boundaries of biomes—by logging in tropical rain forests and taiga, by polluting the atmosphere and oceans, and through global warming. You can help protect the planet by learning about its amazing diversity of life, and by going out into the natural world and experiencing it with wonder and appreciation. Whether for a school project or just for fun, this book will help you learn about ecology, biology, and science in general in a hands-on way. Get messy, have fun, and remember these safety tips:

1. Be sure you have an adult's permission before starting any experiment.
2. Before starting any experiment, read directions carefully and assemble all supplies.
3. Some thermometers contain mercury, which is a toxic metal. If you have a mercury thermometer, ask your parents to take it to a thermometer exchange location, where they can trade it in for a safer model.

*A postman butterfly sips nectar from a lantana flower in a tropical rain forest.*

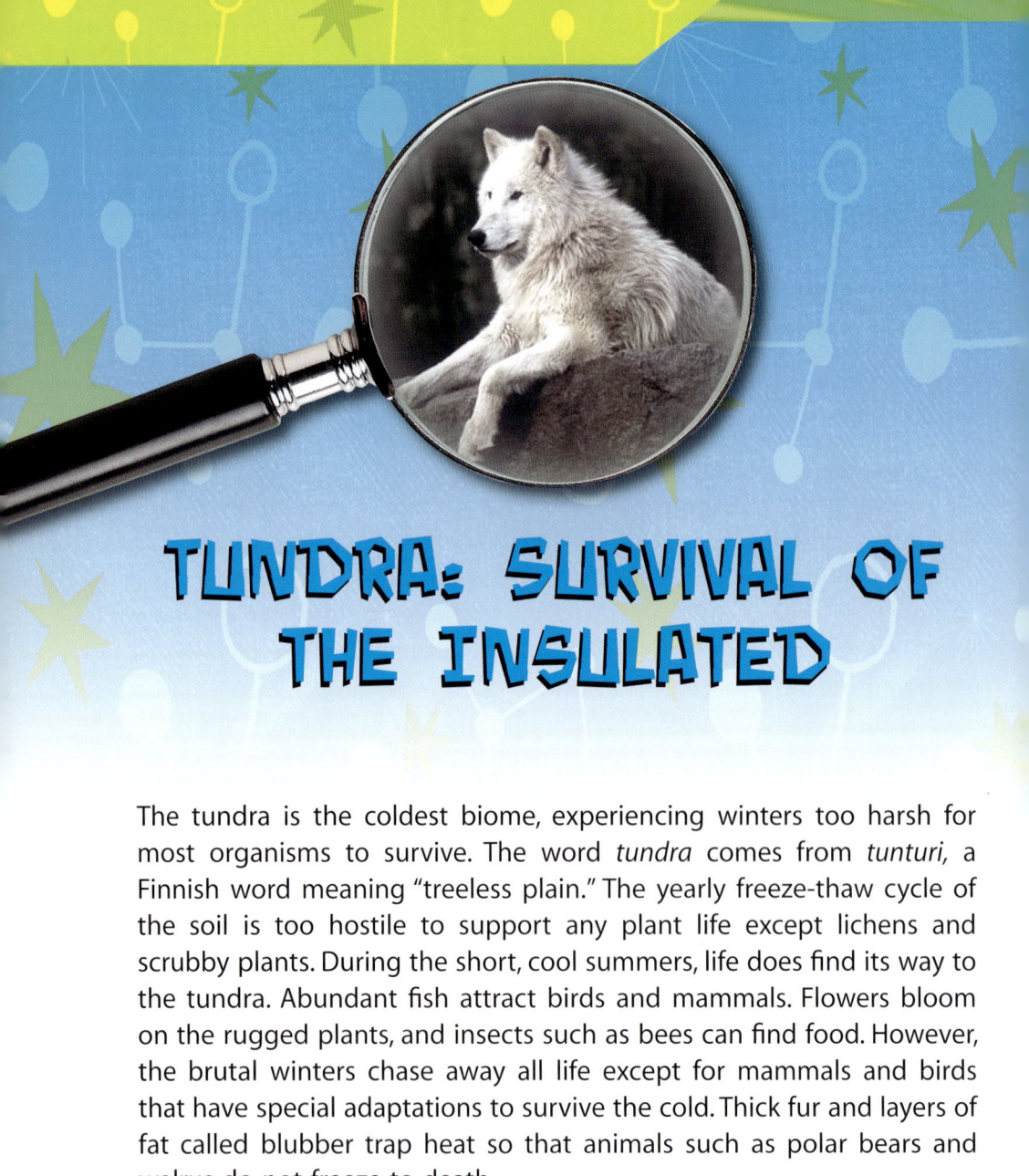

# TUNDRA: SURVIVAL OF THE INSULATED

The tundra is the coldest biome, experiencing winters too harsh for most organisms to survive. The word *tundra* comes from *tunturi,* a Finnish word meaning "treeless plain." The yearly freeze-thaw cycle of the soil is too hostile to support any plant life except lichens and scrubby plants. During the short, cool summers, life does find its way to the tundra. Abundant fish attract birds and mammals. Flowers bloom on the rugged plants, and insects such as bees can find food. However, the brutal winters chase away all life except for mammals and birds that have special adaptations to survive the cold. Thick fur and layers of fat called blubber trap heat so that animals such as polar bears and walrus do not freeze to death.

In this experiment, you can investigate different strategies used in the animal world to keep body heat from escaping.

## MATERIALS
* 2 one-quart (1-liter) glass jars
* 2 thermometers
* 2 boxes slightly larger than the jars (such as cube-style tissue boxes)
* insulating materials such as cotton balls, fleece, wool, craft feathers, craft fur, and solid fat (butter, shortening, or lard)
* **an adult**
* hot water
* science notebook and pen
* refrigerator or freezer

## PROCEDURE
1. Set a thermometer inside each of two 1-quart jars, and then place each jar in a separate box.
2. In one box, fill the space between the jar and the box with one type of insulating material. This box will be the experimental box. Leave the space in the other box empty; this will be your control.
3. With **an adult's** help, fill the jars with hot water. Record the starting temperature, and then again at ten-minute intervals for one hour.
4. Repeat steps 2 and 3 using a different insulating material in the experimental box. Save the solid fat for last, so you can throw the box away when you are done.
5. Compare your results. Which insulating material kept the water the hottest? Which lost the most amount of heat?
6. Take the experiment further by setting it up in the refrigerator, freezer, or outside on a cold day. How well do the insulators perform under chilly conditions?

# TAIGA: LAND OF THE CONIFER

The largest biome in the world, the taiga covers major regions of Canada, northern Europe, and Asia. The taiga is characterized by very cold winters, with average temperatures of −65°F (−54°C). However, summers can reach highs of 70°F (21°C), warm enough to support a wide variety of birds and insect life.

Thick, lush evergreen forests define this biome. This is why the taiga biome is sometimes called the boreal forest (*boreal* means "northern"). Needle-leafed conifer trees are perfectly adapted to thrive there. The leaf size and thick leaf coating enable the trees to survive bitterly cold temperatures where other, broader leaves would simply freeze and die. Days in winter can be as short as six hours, but conifers keep their leaves so that, when spring does come with its long days, they are ready to use them to collect the sun's energy.

Investigate how the conifer has adapted to its environment with the following experiments.

## Materials
* fresh conifer leaves
* fresh deciduous leaves
* scale
* magnifying glass
* freezer
* baking sheet
* aluminum foil
* oven
* oven mitts
* **an adult**

## Procedure
1. Examine the leaves of a conifer tree and a deciduous tree with a magnifying glass. They are obviously different in shape and size, but what else do you notice about them? Look at their coating, color, and veins, for example. When taken all together, do you think the conifer has more or less total leaf mass than the deciduous tree? Write your guess in your science notebook.
2. Cut fresh conifer leaves and deciduous leaves off their trees and weigh them. Gather a roughly equal weight of each type. Record this weight; it is the "wet weight."
3. Divide your leaf collections in half. Place one half of both types of leaves on a baking sheet, and put the baking sheet in the freezer. Leave them overnight.
4. Preheat an oven to 250°F (120°C). Place the remaining leaves on a second baking sheet. With oven mitts and **an adult's** help, place the baking sheet in the oven and bake the leaves for about an hour, or until they look dry and brittle and all the water has baked out of them.

**Exploring Earth's Biomes**

5. Using oven mitts, remove the leaves from the oven and weigh them. This is the "dry weight." Subtract the dry weight from the wet weight (step 2) to get the total weight of water the leaves contained when they were fresh off the tree. To get the percent water, divide the water weight by the wet weight and multiply by 100.
6. Repeat steps 4 and 5 with the frozen leaves in the morning.
7. Compare the water content of the conifer leaves to that of the deciduous leaves. Which leaves hold more water? Why?

# Taiga: Land of the Conifer

**MATERIALS**
- pinecones (woody-looking, not green)
- bowl of water
- towel
- hair dryer (optional)

1. Place a few pinecones in a bowl of water, thoroughly soaking them. Watch the drenched pinecones for about 15 minutes and take notes about what you see. What happens?
2. Remove the pinecones from the water and place them on a towel in a warm spot to dry. If you like, you can speed the drying process with a hair dryer. What happens?
3. How do you think this behavior helps the pine tree survive?

# Rain Forest: Competition

Hot and wet all year round, tropical rain forests are the ideal environments for plants to thrive. Though tropical rain forests cover only 6 percent of the earth's land, they support the widest variety of plant and animal life on earth. Tropical rain forests lie between special latitude lines called the Tropic of Capricorn (about 23.5 degrees South) and the Tropic of Cancer (about 23.5 degrees North). These latitudes receive the most direct sunlight on the planet, bringing the hottest temperatures. However, rain forests also occur in temperate regions, such as the Pacific Northwest in the United States and the west coast of New Zealand. Temperate rain forests have milder temperatures, but because they rarely freeze, many species of plants flourish there year round.

Rain forest plants develop special strategies for getting what they need. The oldest, strongest trees have fought their way through the thick plant life to the sky, where they form the emergent layer. Very tall trees reach the top of the rain forest and spread out their limbs to catch the abundant year-round sunlight on their leaves, forming a living roof to the rain forest called the canopy. The canopy blocks out almost all

## Materials

* 5 flat black plastic seed trays, approximately 10 inches by 20 inches (available at garden centers)
* 1 bag of potting soil
* metal spoon
* marigold seeds
* birdseed
* tablespoon
* craft sticks
* permanent marker or pencil
* spray bottle with water
* ruler
* knife
* **an adult**
* kitchen scale

light to the understory, the middle layer of the forest, but the moisture allows shade-loving plants like ferns and shrubs to thrive. The forest floor teems with bacteria and insect life, which quickly digest dead leaves, plants, and roots, releasing their nutrients to feed the roots of living plants.

Because plants grow so quickly, they are in constant competition for soil, water, and sunlight. Many plants die because there simply aren't enough resources to go around. Study the effects of competition on plant growth, using marigold seeds as a model.

## Procedure

1. Using a spoon, fill the seed trays with potting soil. Reserve some soil for later. Tap the bottoms of the trays gently against a table to firm up the soil, but still keep it loose.
2. Label one craft stick TRAY 1: CONTROL and place it in the dirt of the first tray. Sow 10 marigold seeds over the control tray. Sprinkle potting soil to cover the seeds and tamp the tray down as before. Water the dirt by misting it with a spray bottle. Place the tray in a protected,

**Exploring Earth's Biomes**

sunny location where it can remain undisturbed for a few weeks. A table in front of a window is ideal. Water your seeds lightly each day with the spray bottle.

3. Repeat step 2 with the other trays, labeling them accordingly, to explore the effect of competition on marigold seeds:
    * Tray 2: Plant 10 marigold seeds and 1 tablespoon of birdseed.
    * Tray 3: Plant 10 marigold seeds. Wait 1 week, then plant 1 tablespoon of birdseed.
    * Tray 4: Plant 1 tablespoon of birdseed. Wait 1 week, then plant 10 marigold seeds.
    * Tray 5: Plant 1 tablespoon of birdseed. Label this tray CONTROL: BIRDSEED.

**Rain Forest: Competition**

*Marigolds*

4. When the first tray of seeds has begun to flower, determine the success of marigold growth. In each tray:
   * Count the number of marigold plants and measure the height of each one. Add up all the heights and determine the average height of the marigolds in each tray by dividing the number of plants by the total plant height.
   * Weigh the plants. With **an adult's** help, cut off each marigold stem at the ground using a knife. Weigh all the harvested plants from each tray together using the kitchen scale.
5. How did competition affect the growth of marigold plants? Compare the height and mass of marigolds in the control tray—where there was no competition for water, sunlight, or soil nutrients—with marigold growth in the other trays. Can you crowd the marigold seeds to the point where they don't grow at all?

Take the experiment further by blocking out some or all of the sunlight from the seedlings, as though they were under a forest canopy.

# Temperate Deciduous Forest: Hibernation

Temperate deciduous forests differ from the other biomes in that they have four clearly defined seasons—spring, summer, winter, and fall—with a regular amount of rainfall throughout the year. Though conifer trees also thrive in this biome, these forests are characterized by deciduous trees, which lose their leaves in the fall. As days begin to shorten at the end of summer, deciduous trees stop producing chlorophyll, a green pigment important for photosynthesis (making sugar from sunlight). As the chlorophyll fades, other pigments remain, leaving the once-green leaves yellow, orange, red, or even purple before they drop from the tree. These beautiful fall colors can be seen throughout the eastern United States, parts of Europe, China, Russia, and Japan.

Animals that live in this biome experience a range of temperatures as the seasons change from hot summers to cold winters and back again. Many animals in temperate regions cope with colder temperatures by hibernating. During hibernation, an animal's breathing and heart rates slow down considerably so that its body uses less energy. Though warm-blooded mammals could survive the colder temperatures for a

**MATERIALS**
* goldfish (from a pet store)
* fishbowl full of water
* small, sealed container of frozen water
* timer or stopwatch
* aquarium thermometer

time, they often hibernate because there is not enough food to survive the winter. Colder temperatures affect cold-blooded animals directly, slowing down their metabolism so that they literally stop moving. Cold-blooded animals instinctively know to protect themselves when temperatures begin to drop by finding a warm, safe place to spend the winter, such as in an underground burrow.

In these short experiments, you can observe the reversible effects of the cold on the behavior of three different kinds of cold-blooded animals. Be careful not to harm the animals in these experiments.

## PROCEDURE: FISH
1. Introduce the goldfish to the bowl, following instructions from the pet store. Give the fish at least a day to get used to its new home.
2. Measure the fish's breathing rate by counting the number of times its gills flap in and out in one minute. Take several measurements and average them to get the most accurate rate.
3. Add the frozen container to the bowl and observe the fish. Note the water temperature and count its breathing rate. Note: Ice cubes will also work, but unless they are made using dechlorinated water, they will contain chemicals that could harm the fish.
4. Remove the frozen container and allow the fishbowl to return to room temperature.

*Exploring Earth's Biomes*

**MATERIALS**
* 2 empty 2-liter bottles
* funnel
* cornstarch
* dirt (dug up with permission or from a garden center)
* worms (dug up with permission or from a bait shop)
* apple peels
* refrigerator

**PROCEDURE: WORMS**

1. Using a funnel, add cornstarch and dirt to two 2-liter bottles in alternating layers until the bottles are about half full. Add the same number of worms to each container. Top the layers with a thin cover of apple peels to give the worms a little food.
2. Set one container in the sun, and the other in the refrigerator. Leave the containers in their spots for a day, checking on them frequently and making notes on their appearance.
3. At the end of the experiment, compare the worms' activity. Are the cornstarch and dirt layers equally mixed between the warm and cool containers? Have the apple peels been eaten?
4. Return the worms to the wild, either in your yard or in a park.

**Temperate Deciduous Forest: Hibernation**

### MATERIALS
* small frog (caught or from a pet store)
* shoebox-sized plastic container with breathing holes in lid
* soft fresh mud, preferably from a pond or riverbank
* timer or stopwatch
* ice cubes
* cup, small enough to stand upright in the container

### PROCEDURE: FROG

1. Fill one corner of a container with fresh mud, making a pile bigger than the frog's body.
2. Place a frog in the container. Observe its breathing rate (watch its neck or the sides of its stomach) and time how many breaths it takes per minute.
3. Fill the cup with ice cubes. Open the container and place the cup in the end opposite the mud.
4. Wait, watch, and take notes. Time the frog's breathing rate as it gets colder inside the habitat. Once the frog is cold enough, it will burrow into the mud to hibernate.
5. Take away the ice cubes. Allow the container to warm up slowly and the frog will come back out.
6. Return a caught frog to the place you found it. If you bought your frog from a pet store, enjoy your new pet!

# GRASSLAND: FIGHTING EROSION

Grasslands found in the central United States, Asia, Argentina, and southern Africa make up about 25 percent of the world's land. They receive between 10 and 50 inches (25 and 125 centimeters) of rain each year, depending on their location. The cold winters and hot summers of this biome are a perfect match for perennial grasses, but also for major crops such as corn and soybeans. Much of the world's produce and livestock are raised in the grasslands, making this biome vital for our food supply.

The roots of perennial grasses keep the soil loose, rich, and extremely fertile. Grasses also protect the soil. Without these grasses, the valuable soil ground can get blown away by the intense prairie winds, or washed away by flash floods. You can observe the effects of grasses on soil erosion with the following experiment.

*Two giraffes on the African savanna, or grassland*

**MATERIALS**
- 12 flat seed trays (10 inches by 20 inches)
- a bag of potting soil
- 3 different kinds of grass seed (wheat, rye, birdseed mix)
- craft sticks or garden markers
- spray bottle
- pencil
- watering can
- electric fan or hair dryer
- extension cord for outdoor use

*Grasslands in the Goorooyarroo Nature Reserve in Australia*

# Exploring Earth's Biomes

## Procedure

1. Loosely fill the twelve trays with potting soil. Tap the bottom of each tray against a flat surface to settle the soil.
2. Sprinkle the surface of three trays with one grass seed type. Label each tray with the grass seed name. To one tray, add the label CONTROL, to the next tray WIND, and to the last tray RAIN. Sprinkle a layer of soil over the seeds and tap each tray down again.
3. Repeat step 2 with the other two grass seed types.
4. Repeat the labeling part of step 2 for the final three trays. Do not plant any seeds in the soil of these trays.
5. Spray all the trays with water, including the trays with no seeds, and set them in a sunny, protected place. Water them daily (including the unseeded tray) and check for growth, making notes of how long it takes. The grasses may grow at different rates; this is fine. They are ready for experimenting when the grass is two to three inches tall.

# Grassland: Fighting Erosion

6. Grasslands can be very windy places. Crops in the American Dust Bowl were ruined in the 1920s when ferocious winds whipped up dry, overused dirt into dust storms. What effect do grasses have on the soil during windstorms? Take the trays marked WIND outside and set them next to each other in a row. Use an electric fan or hair dryer to create fierce winds on all four trays at the same time. Keep the storm going until you see dirt flying from at least one of the trays. Put the electrical equipment away.
7. Take the trays marked RAIN outside and set them next to each other in a row. Water them all equally using a watering can from above to simulate a rainstorm. Keep going until you see major changes in the dirt in at least one tray.
8. Compare and contrast the effects of the different grass types. Which one held the soil together the best through the rain? The wind? How did the unplanted soil differ from the grassy soil during the storms?

*A cornfield in the Midwest gets fertilized.*

# DESERT: THIRSTY PLANTS

Deserts are the driest biome, receiving less than 10 inches (25 centimeters) of rainfall each year. Some deserts go for several years without any precipitation at all. The driest spots in the Atacama Desert in Chile have waited over 400 years for a drop of rain!* These wastelands cover 20 percent of the planet's surface, though not all are sandy dune fields. In fact, the largest desert in the world is the 5.4 million-square-mile (14 million-square-kilometer) continent of Antarctica, on which less than 8 inches (20 centimeters) of rain falls annually.

Although we often think of sandy deserts as hot, in fact the danger of deserts is that they take temperature to the extreme. Because deserts have few plants to trap moisture near the ground, the heat of the sun determines their temperature. In most deserts, these conditions bring scorching hot days that lead to freezing cold nights. With so few plants and such wide-ranging temperatures, it's no wonder that few animals live in the desert.

*Extreme Science: "Driest Place: Atacama Desert, Chile," http://www.extremescience.com/zoom/index.php/driest-desert

**MATERIALS**
* a healthy potted succulent houseplant, such as a jade plant, aloe, or Christmas cactus (found in garden centers)
* a non-succulent houseplant
* magnifying glass
* digital camera (optional)
* scale
* kitchen
* oven
* **an adult**
* baking sheet
* aluminum foil
* oven mitts

*Christmas cactus*

Because there is limited rainfall in a desert, the soil must be highly nutritious. Only specialized plants called succulents can grow in desert sand. These plants trap water in their leaves or trunks, and they have waxy coatings to keep the water from evaporating through their skin. Investigate how these unique plants hoard water with the following experiment.

**PROCEDURE**
1. Cut a leaf off each houseplant and study it carefully under a magnifying glass. Describe any special characteristics or structures in your notebook or, better yet, take pictures with a digital camera.
2. Water the two houseplants until the soil is visibly wet. Wait four hours, then cut a leaf off each one. Look at each leaf carefully with the magnifying glass and/or take another picture. What effect did watering have on them?
3. Preheat an oven to 250°F (120°C). Line a baking sheet with aluminum foil.

**Exploring Earth's Biomes**

non-succulent

succulent

4. Cut leaves from the succulent plant and weigh them. You may have to cut 10 or more leaves to get a significant weight. Record the weight of these leaves. Then cut about an equal weight of leaves from the non-succulent plant, and record that weight. The weight of each group of fresh leaves is its wet weight.

### Desert: Thirsty Plants

5. Place the leaves on the lined baking sheet and, with the help of **an adult**, bake in the preheated oven for an hour, or until the leaves look very dry.
6. Now weigh each type of leaf. This is the dry weight. Subtract the wet weight from the dry weight to know how much the water weighed in the original leaves. Find out what percentage of the original leaf was water by dividing the dry weight by the wet weight. Which type of leaf held the most water? What advantage would that give the leaf in its natural habitat?
7. Now for the desert test. This is the easiest experiment of all—ignore your houseplants. Watch them and take notes or pictures of them each day. How long can they go without water until each one begins to wilt and turn brown?

# Biomes in a Bag

Now that you've learned about each of the major land biomes, you can create your own biome to fit on your windowsill!

### Materials
* clear 2-liter bottle, cut in half
* gallon-size zip-top storage bag
* aquarium gravel
* potting soil
* birdseed
* water

### Procedure
1. Set the bottom half of a 2-liter bottle upright in a zip-top storage bag.
2. Make a layer of gravel ½ inch (1 centimeter) deep in the bottle. Add a 1-inch (2.5-centimeter) layer of potting soil over the gravel. Tap the bottom of the bottle against a hard surface to level the layers and pack them a bit.

3. Sprinkle the birdseed on the soil surface, then cover the seeds with a sprinkling of potting soil. Tap the bottle again to pack the soil against the seeds, but still keep it loose.
4. Gently water the soil until you see water in the gravel. Seal the top of the zip-top bag.
5. Find a sunny spot for your biome, such as a windowsill. Watch it every day and take notes on what you see happening.

Take your experiment further. Create a biome-in-a-bag for each of the six categories of biomes described in this book and investigate what happens in the different growing conditions. For example: a tropical rain forest is hot and wet, but dark. Set up a biome, add more water than you did in step 4, place it in a warm spot, and cover it with a light towel. To set up a taiga experiment, create a biome that is wet and keep it cool by surrounding it with ice packs or cool wet towels. How would you set up a desert? A temperate deciduous forest? A grassland?

# Hula Hoop Biomes

You have seen how biomes are classified on a global scale by climate and geography. But in biology, scale is relative. In your own backyard, an ecologist could identify dozens of biomes—under a tree, in a puddle, in a garden, on the porch—any area that defines a unique set of living conditions.

Use the following experiment to study plant and animal populations that make up mini-biomes in your area.

### Materials
* city map
* yard or park
* **an adult**
* hula hoop
* magnifying glass
* handheld shovel
* binoculars
* field guides for your area—birds, insects, spiders, mammals, reptiles, and amphibians
* notebook and pencil

**PROCEDURE**

1. Identify a spot in your town or city where two different kinds of mini-biomes meet, such as the edge of the woods, a riverbank, or where a park meets the pavement. You may already know a great place. If not, look at a map of your city to get some ideas. Have **an adult** accompany you to your chosen field site.

2. In your notebook, label the two biomes—for example, the woods (biome A) and a mown grass field (biome B). Toss your hula hoop into biome A so that it lands on the ground in a random place. Carefully examine the ground inside your hula hoop, taking detailed notes about what lives there. Describe the number and characteristics of plants, mosses, and/or fungi. Spend at least 15 minutes with your hoop to observe insects that crawl in and out. Things that are over and under the hoop count, too. Look above you and count birds, lizards, or tree-dwelling mammals, using binoculars if you need to. Dig up the soil a bit and see what kinds of worms, grubs, or bugs live below. Consult field guides to identify your finds. Also, make general notes about how much sunshine, wind, or precipitation you detect at the hula hoop site.

# Exploring Earth's Biomes

3. Repeat step 2 twice for biome A, so that you have a sample of three hula hoop tosses. This way, you are sure to get a good sample of organisms for your records.
4. Repeat step 2 three times for biome B.
5. Repeat step 2 three times for the border between biomes A and B.
6. Compare and contrast your findings for biomes A, B, and their intersection. All three mini-biomes experience the same climate, so how and why are the plant and animal populations different? What other factors influence plant and animal populations at your field site?

Ecologists are often concerned with biodiversity within a biome. When many different species live in the same area, it indicates a healthy ecosystem with abundant food resources. Fewer species can indicate an ecosystem in trouble. Which hula hoop sampling group had the greatest number of different species identified, and why?

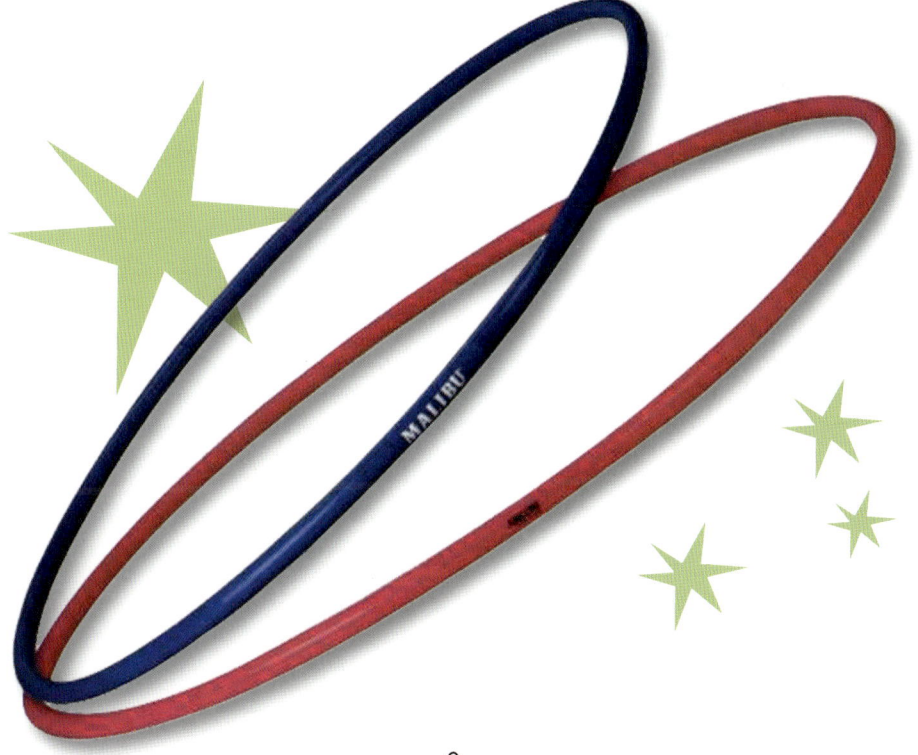

# Food Web: Where Does Your Dinner Come From?

All living things need energy to survive. Plants get their energy from the sun, turning carbon dioxide and water into sugars using photosynthesis. All life on earth depends on photosynthesis. For this reason, ecologists refer to plants as producers and animals as consumers. Since animals cannot make their own food, they rely on plants to do it for them. Producers can be as tiny as phytoplankton floating in the ocean, or as large as a redwood tree. Herbivores, or animals that eat only plants, are primary consumers. This group includes livestock such as cows and sheep, and important insect species such as bees. Carnivores that eat herbivores are secondary consumers. Spiders are secondary consumers, as are frogs and tigers. Carnivores that eat other carnivores are tertiary consumers. An alligator, which eats carnivorous fish, is an example of a tertiary consumer. Humans can be primary, secondary, or tertiary consumers.

A food web illustrates how energy from plants passes throughout a biome by linking the eaters and the eaten. The web begins with plants, which link to herbivores. Herbivores link to secondary or tertiary consumers. Each member of the biome provides food for another

**MATERIALS**
* paper
* pencil
* colored pencils
* computer with Internet and printer access
* magazines
* scissors
* glue
* yarn
* poster board

member, until the top consumer—which eats but is not eaten—is reached. Because most animals must eat more than one kind of food to survive, the links often interconnect to form a web.

Human food webs are unique in that our diets are not restricted to our local biomes. We can transport food all over the world. Explore the concept of food webs by creating one for the ultimate consumer—you.

## PROCEDURE
1. What did you eat for dinner last night? Title a separate piece of paper with the name of each dish. For example, use three sheets of paper to chart your meal of "pepperoni pizza," "salad," and "milk."
2. Underneath the title, list the ingredients that made up each part of the meal. If your meal came from a box, use the ingredients listed on the box. If you ate out, call the restaurant and ask to know specifically what went into making your meal. Interview your mom or dad for answers if they cooked your dinner.

**Exploring Earth's Biomes**

3. Consider each ingredient carefully. Write down the plant or animal sources from which it came. Flour to make pizza crust, for example, comes from wheat. Pepperoni can be made from pork, beef, or a combination of the two.
4. Underline your sources in green if they are producers, in orange if they are consumers. If you consumed something from a consumer—which you did if you ate meat, fish, eggs, or dairy—research what that consumer eats. Look it up on the Internet, or better yet, call a local livestock farmer and ask. Add those sources to your chart, drawing lines to connect them to the consumer source.
5. For a nice presentation, display your research on poster board with pictures of each of the sources of your dinner, both producer and consumer, printing them or clipping them from magazines. Connect consumers to the producer sources of their diet with yarn.
6. Research the distance each of your food sources had to travel to get to your dinner table. All that transportation creates a lot of pollution in the form of burned truck or tanker fuel. Use a carbon footprint calculator like the Low Carbon Diet calculator (http://eatlowcarbon.org) to find out how many tons of carbon dioxide your meal cost the planet. Can you make changes in your diet to lower your carbon footprint?

**Food Web**

Take this project further. Pick your favorite animal and research what it eats—and what eats it—using the Internet or the library. Create a food web for it and its biome using the same steps as above.

# MICROBE FOOD WEB: CREATE A WINOGRADSKY COLUMN

Bacteria and single-celled plants and animals work invisibly to make life possible in every world biome. Phytoplankton—single-celled plants and photosynthetic bacteria that live in aquatic biomes—are the single most important group of producers on the planet. Consumer bacteria feed on plant and animal waste, cleaning up the ecosystem and recycling nutrients. These organisms work together to create the chemistry a pond needs to support plant and animal life.

In one spoonful of pond mud lives an entire microscopic world of producers and consumers. Normally these organisms are too small and intermixed to be observed without a microscope. However, Russian microbiologist Sergei Winogradsky discovered that different types of bacteria would grow in colorful layers if they were placed in a cylindrical container of pond mud and water.

A Winogradsky column creates a self-sufficient environment for a number of colorful microorganisms. Aerobic bacteria and algae form a familiar green layer at the top, where they receive the most sunlight for photosynthesis and create oxygen. Anaerobic bacteria need a low-oxygen environment and settle at the bottom in the pond mud. They

## Materials

- 5 cups of mud from a pond or stream (the stinkier, the better!)
- 5 cups water (preferably from an outdoor source)
- 1 egg
- mixing bowl
- metal spoon
- two sheets of newspaper
- 1 tablespoon powdered chalk
- funnel
- clear plastic 2-liter bottle
- aluminum foil
- rubber band

create hydrogen sulfide gas in their energy-making process. Different species of other pond microbes require different levels of hydrogen sulfide and oxygen, so they settle somewhere in the middle, where the chemistry best suits them. For example, green sulfur bacteria can handle higher levels of hydrogen sulfide than purple sulfur bacteria, so the green bacteria form a layer closer to the pond mud than the purple bacteria do.

Your Winogradsky column will take several weeks to develop, but it will make an impressive display because the pond bacteria settle out in colorful layers according to their food needs.

**Be sure to go with an adult when collecting samples from the pond.**

## Procedure

1. Remove sticks and rocks from the mud to make it as smooth as possible. Pour the pond mud and an egg into a mixing bowl. Slowly add water until you can stir the mixture, but it is still thick. You may

have water left over. Shred the newspaper, then add it and the powdered chalk to the mud mixture. Stir thoroughly.
2. Funnel a few spoonfuls of the mud mixture into a bottle. Tap the bottom of the bottle firmly against your work surface to dislodge trapped air bubbles. Repeat until the bottle is about 90 percent full. Let the bottle sit for 30 minutes to allow the mud to settle. After that time, the bottle should have a 1-inch (2-centimeter) layer of water at the top. If not, add or remove water so that it has an appropriately deep layer of water.

# Microbe Food Web

3. Cap the bottle with aluminum foil, and secure it with a rubber band. Set your newly made Winogradsky column in a windowsill or other location where it can receive indirect sunlight.
4. Watch your column over the next few weeks, taking notes each day. Measure the height of the different layers, noting colors that develop as the bacterial populations grow.
5. Research the names of the different organisms that grow in your column, and find out why they are thriving. Make a food web for the microorganisms. What do they eat, and what eats them? What are their roles in a pond environment? What would happen to the pond if they died out?

# FURTHER READING

## Books
Brinkley, Edward S. *National Wildlife Federation Field Guide to Birds of North America.* New York: Sterling, 2007.
DK Publishing. *Nature Explorer.* New York: DK Publishing, 2010.
Evans, Arthur. *National Wildlife Federation Field Guide to Insects, Spiders, and Related Species of North America.* New York: Sterling, 2007.
Kershner, Bruce. *National Wildlife Federation Field Guide to Trees of North America.* New York: Sterling, 2008.
Lantham, Donna. *Amazing Biome Projects You Can Build Yourself.* White River Junction, VT: Nomad Press, 2009.
Rothschild, David. *Earth Matters.* New York: DK Publishing, 2008.
VanCleave, Janice. *Janice Van Cleave's Science Around the World: Activities on Biomes from Pole to Pole.* Hoboken, NJ: John Wiley & Sons, 2004.

## On the Internet
Exploring the Environment—Biomes
    http://www.cotf.edu/ete/modules/msese/earthsysflr/biomes.html
Missouri Botanical Garden—What's It Like Where You Live?
    http://www.mbgnet.net/index.html
NASA Earth Observatory—Mission: Biomes
    http://earthobservatory.nasa.gov/Experiments/Biome/
The Wild Classroom—Biomes of the World
    http://www.thewildclassroom.com/biomes/index.html
WorldBiomes.com—Explore Five of the World's Main Biomes
    http://www.worldbiomes.com/

**PHOTO CREDITS:** Cover, pp. 1, 4–6, 8, 10, 14, 16–18, 23–26, 36, 44—CreativeCommons 2.0; All other photos—Claire O'Neal. Every effort has been made to locate all copyright holders of material used in this book. If any errors or omissions have occurred, corrections will be made in future editions of the book.

# FURTHER READING

**Works Consulted**

Bodonsky, Deborah, Amberlee Chaussee, and Bonnie Samuelson. "NASA Quest: Building a Winogradsky Column." National Aeronautics and Space Administration Ames Research Center. http://quest.nasa.gov/projects/astrobiology/fieldwork/lessons/Winogradsky_5_8.pdf

Botkin, Daniel B., and Edward A. Keller. *Environmental Science: Earth as a Living Planet* (Fourth Edition). Hoboken, New Jersey: John Wiley & Sons, Inc., 2003.

Campbell, Neil A. *Biology.* Menlo Park, CA: The Benjamin/Cummings Publishing Company, Inc., 1996.

Chinery, Michael. *Life in the Wild: Animal Survival.* London: Lorenz Books, 2005.

Dashefsky, H. Steven. *Environmental Science: High School Science Fair Experiments.* Blue Ridge Summit, PA: TAB Books, 1994.

Holmes, Martha, and Mike Gunton. *Life: Extraordinary Animals, Extreme Behavior.* Berkeley, CA: University of California Press, 2010.

Lee, Ellen, et al. *American Field Guide.* Oregon Public Broadcasting and PBS. http://www.pbs.org/americanfieldguide/

New Mexico Outdoor Classroom Program. "Habitats on the Edge." http://www.emnrd.state.nm.us/PRD/documents/HabitatinaHoop_FEB2010_000.pdf

PBS Kids. "Biome in a Baggie." http://pbskids.org/zoom/activities/sci/biomeinabaggie.html

Pullen, Stephanie, and Kacey Ballard. *UCMP: The World's Biomes.* http://www.ucmp.berkeley.edu/glossary/gloss5/biome/

Schmidt-Nielsen, Knut. *Animal Physiology: Adaptation and Environment.* New York: Cambridge University Press, 1983.

U.S. Geological Survey. "Lessons on the Lake: Activity—Bird Beak Buffet." http://pubs.usgs.gov/of/1998/of98-805/lessons/chpt2/act5.htm

Woodward, Susan L. *Biomes of Earth: Terrestrial, Aquatic, and Human-Dominated.* Santa Barbara, California: Greenwood Press, 2003.

# GLOSSARY

**adaptation** (aa-dap-TAY-shun)—A physical change that helps a living thing survive in a new environment.
**aerobic bacteria** (ayr-OH-bik bak-TEER-ee-uh)—Single-celled organisms that use oxygen to survive.
**anaerobic bacteria** (AN-uh-roh-bik bak-TEER-ee-uh)—Single-celled organisms that live in an environment that has no oxygen.
**biodiversity** (by-oh-dih-VER-sih-tee)—The number and variety of living things found within a given area.
**canopy** (KAH-nuh-pee)—An open, sheltering cover, like an umbrella. In a rain forest, the canopy is the second-tallest layer of life.
**chlorophyll** (KLOR-uh-fil)—Green pigment found in plants and photosynthetic bacteria that harnesses energy from light.
**conifer** (KAH-nih-fer)—A type of tree or shrub that keeps its leaves year-round, such as pine or fir trees; conifer leaves are usually needle- or scale-shaped.
**consumer** (kun-SOO-mer)—An organism that uses other organisms for food.
**deciduous** (deh-SID-joo-us)—A type of tree or shrub that sheds its leaves in autumn, such as maple or oak; deciduous leaves are usually flat and broad.
**ecologist** (ee-KAH-luh-jist)—A biologist who studies how living things interact with their environment.
**emergent** (ee-MER-jent) **layer**—The tallest layer of life in a rain forest, which reaches through ("emerges" from) the canopy.
**extinction** (ek-STINK-shun)—When no more individuals of a species are alive.
**forest floor**—The ground underneath a forest, where dead animals, dead plant matter, and scavengers such as insects and bacteria gather.
**hibernate** (HY-ber-nayt)—To rest through the winter, usually by slowing down the metabolism.
**latitude** (LAT-ih-tood)—The distance north or south of the equator, measured in degrees. All points along the same line of latitude receive equal amounts of yearly sunshine.
**metabolism** (meh-TAB-buh-lizm)—The processes needed to provide a living thing with energy, including digestion, circulation of the blood, and breathing.
**perennial** (pur-EH-nee-ul)—Coming back several years in a row.
**photosynthesis** (foh-toh-SIN-theh-sis)—The biological process by which plants and certain kinds of bacteria create sugars from the sun, water, and carbon dioxide.
**photosynthetic bacteria** (foh-toh-sin-THEH-tik bak-TEER-ee-uh)—Single-celled organisms that produce their own energy using chlorophyll.
**primary consumer** (PRY-mayr-ee kun-SOO-mer)—An organism that gets energy from eating plants or photosynthetic bacteria.
**producer** (proh-DOO-ser)—An organism that makes its own food energy (such as plants).
**secondary consumer** (SEH-kun-dayr-ee kun-SOO-mer)—An organism that gets all or part of its energy by eating primary consumers.
**succulent** (SUK-yoo-lunt)—Any type of plant native to dry climates that stores water in its leaves and trunk.
**tertiary consumer** (TER-shee-ayr-ee kun-SOO-mer)—An organism that gets all or part of its energy by eating secondary consumers.
**understory** (UN-der-stor-ee)—The dark middle layer of a rain forest below the canopy and above the forest floor.

# INDEX

adaptations  7, 8, 10
aerobic bacteria  40
anaerobic bacteria  40
Antarctica  6, 26
aquatic biomes  6, 40
Arctic Circle  5
Asia  10
Atacama Desert  26
biome in a bag  30–31
blubber  8
boreal forest  10 (*and see* taiga)
Canada  5, 10
canopy  14, 17
carbon footprint  38
China  5
chlorophyll  18
competition  14–17
conifer  5, 10–13, 18
consumer  36–39, 40
deciduous  5, 6, 11–13, 18, 31
desert  6, 26–29, 31
diversity  5, 7, 35
ecologist  7, 32, 35, 36
emergent layer  14
Europe  5, 10, 18
extinction  6
food web  36–39, 40–43
forest floor  15
frog  21, 36
global warming  7
goldfish  18–19
grassland  5–6, 22–25, 31
habitat  21, 29

hibernation  18–21
houseplants  27–29
hula hoop biomes  32–35
human impact  7, 37–39
insulation  7–8
Japan  5, 18
marigold  15–17
marmot  4
mini-biome  32–35
mountain goat  4
mountain lion  4
New Zealand  5, 14
Pacific Northwest, U.S.  5, 14
photosynthesis  18, 36, 40
photosynthetic bacteria  40
pinecones  13
pollution  7
Russia  5, 6, 18, 40
South Africa  5
succulents  27–29
taiga  5, 6, 7, 10–13, 31
temperate deciduous forest  5, 6, 18–21, 31
temperate rain forest  5, 6, 14
thermometer  7, 9, 19
tropical rain forest  5, 6, 7, 14–17, 31
Tropic of Cancer  6, 14
Tropic of Capricorn  6, 14
tundra  4–5, 6, 8–9
understory  14
United States  5, 14, 18, 22
Winogradsky column  40–43
worms  20, 33

# About the Author

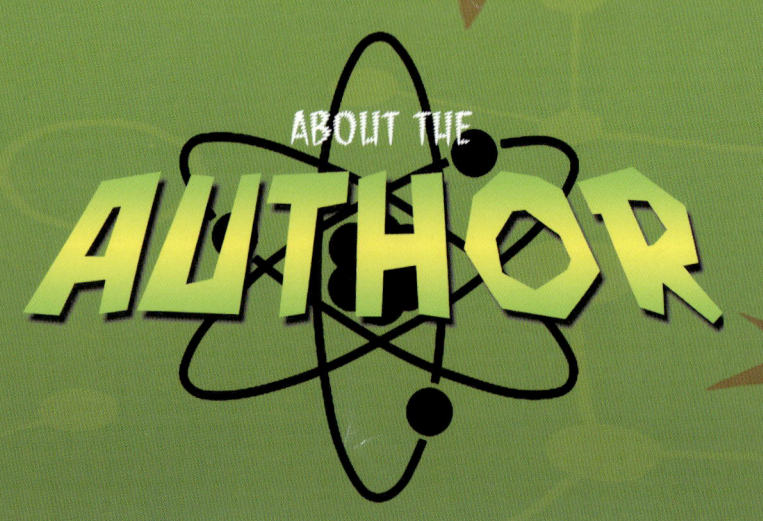

Claire O'Neal has written over a dozen books for Mitchell Lane Publishers, including *Projects in Genetics* in this series and *Volcanoes, Earthquakes,* and *Rocks and Minerals* in the series Earth Science Projects for Kids. She holds degrees in English and Biology from Indiana University, and a Ph.D. in Chemistry from the University of Washington. She lives in Delaware with her husband, two young sons, and a fat black cat. Though she has lived in a temperate deciduous forest most of her life, her favorite biome is the temperate rain forest.